P9-DHE-233

Young Lancelot

To Roland Nelson with thanks for being, quite simply,
the best friend one could hope for
—R.S.S.

For Bob and Ruth
—J.H.

Young Lancelot

by Robert D. San Souci

illustrated by Jamichael Henterly

A Doubleday Book for Young Readers

ong ago, in northern France, good King Ban and Queen Helen ruled the kingdom of Benwick. They had a beautiful baby son named Lancelot.

King Ban was at war with wicked King Claudas, whose army had laid siege to Ban's city and castle of Trebe.

King Ban sent messengers to his ally, King Arthur, across the sea in Britain, begging for help. But Arthur was beset by his own enemies and had no knights to spare for King Ban.

Queen Helen said to her husband, "We must go ourselves to Camelot. Surely Arthur will help if we ask him in person."

Ban agreed. While the queen prepared herself and tiny Lancelot for the journey, he spoke to his lords. "Upon your honor, do not let Claudas discover I have gone, or he will redouble his attacks."

"We promise," his men answered.

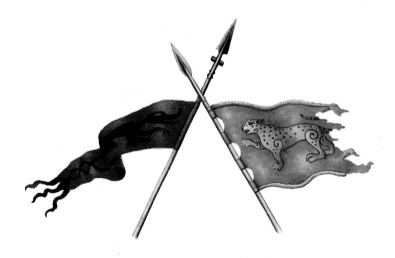

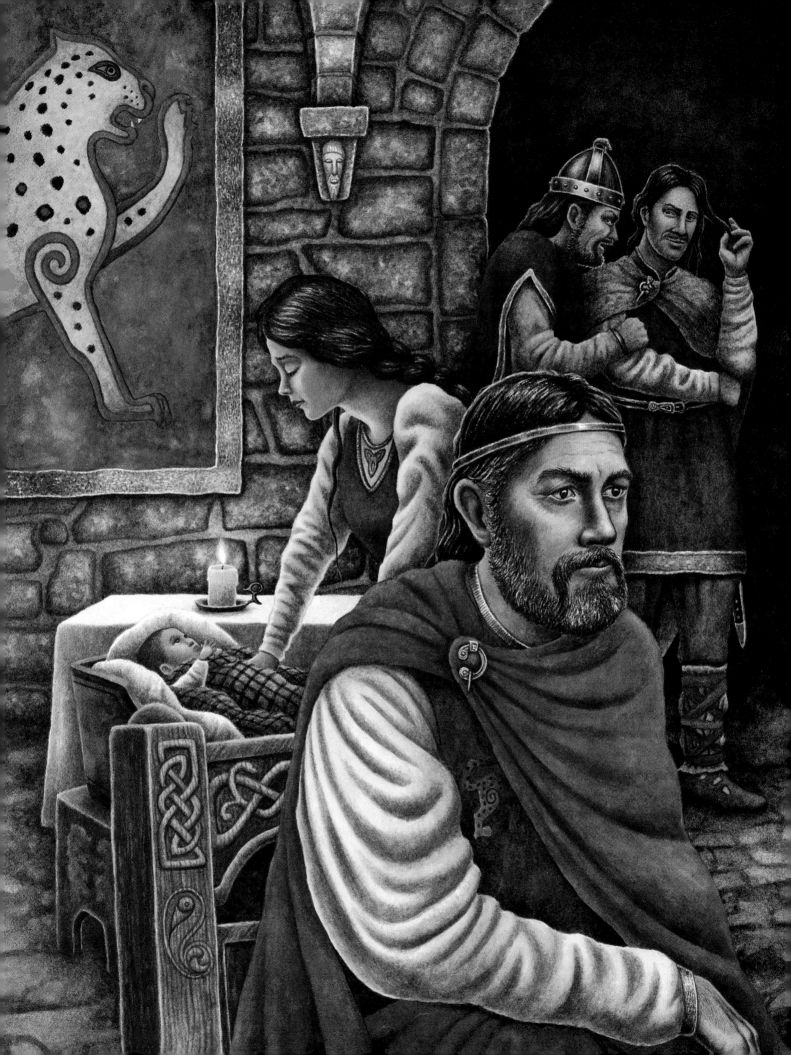

That night the king and queen took Lancelot and secretly left the castle. They rode at breakneck speed through the forest. At dawn they rested beside a wooded lake at the foot of a high hill. Queen Helen slept with her baby in a basket beside her. King Ban, eager for a last glimpse of his beloved Trebe, rode to the hilltop.

To his horror, he saw the city and castle ablaze. "I have been betrayed by those I trusted most!" he cried. His heart broken, the king tumbled from his horse, which bolted down the hill.

Helen saw Ban's riderless horse. Leaving her sleeping child, she ran up the hill. When she found her husband dead, she wailed so loudly that the hill and the wide lake echoed with the sound. Then she fell lifeless beside him.

As the echoes of her cry faded, the lake waters parted. A tall, handsome woman, with golden hair and pale skin, walked onto the shore. She picked up the orphaned child and kissed him. Then she turned and walked back into the water.

The stranger was Niniane, the Lady of the Lake, a powerful enchantress. The lake was a magic illusion, hiding a deep valley filled with gardens and orchards. At its heart was a splendid palace where Niniane lived, surrounded by knights and ladies-in-waiting. To them the waters of the lake seemed nothing more than blue-green mist.

Niniane told no one the child's name, which she discovered through magic. She also learned many things about his past and his destiny. She gave him into the keeping of a nurse, who asked, "How shall I call him, Lady?"

"Call him King's Son," replied Niniane, "and treat him kindly, for I love him as my own child."

So he grew up knowing only the name King's Son and thinking Niniane was his mother. When he asked, "Who is my father and what is my true name?" she replied, "I will tell you when you claim your destiny as the greatest knight of the greatest king."

In that magic place, the boy grew rapidly into a handsome, robust, and intelligent lad. Niniane gave him a tutor who taught him how to read and write and conduct himself as a gentleman. Her knights taught the boy how to ride and use spear, sword, and bow. He strove to excel in all these things, because he knew that a knight must balance the arts of courtly life with the arts of battle.

But as the pet of Niniane's court, he grew up arrogant and cold. Niniane was troubled. "A knight needs two hearts," she told him. "One should be hard as a diamond when battling cruelty and injustice. The other should be soft as warm wax to respond to goodness and gentleness."

Lancelot scoffed at the idea of a knight moved by tenderness. "A warrior must be strong inside and out," he insisted. "I want only a heart that is diamond-hard."

When Lancelot heard of King Arthur and his knights, he begged Niniane, "Send me to Camelot, where I can be knighted by Arthur and become a champion of the Round Table."

His guardian sighed. "You are not yet ready, King's Son."

"You yourself say this is my destiny. Yet you hold me back," he said angrily. "How can you be so unkind?"

"Oh, King's Son," she said tearfully. "Though it breaks my heart to part from you, I will send you to King Arthur."

Niniane provided him with armor, a helmet, and a shield

all of silver. She gave him a sword with a blade that would never dull and a lance with a silver tip. Finally she presented him with a snow-white horse that had trappings of silver and white.

When he was ready to depart, he asked Niniane, "One final gift I beg of you: What is my true name?"

"Before I can reveal this to you, you must prove yourself the greatest knight of all," she said. "Tell King Arthur that you are sent by the Lady of the Lake, and he will welcome you."

So the young man traveled to Camelot. There Arthur greeted him warmly, dubbed him Knight of the Lake, and invited him to sit at the Round Table with the other champions.

Lancelot's arrogance and hard-heartedness made him more enemies than friends at court. But he was concerned only with gaining glory and claiming his rightful name.

He pleaded with Arthur, "Set me the hardest tasks you can. Let me prove myself worthy of my place at the Round Table."

"Very well," said Arthur. "Two matters weigh most heavily on me. The first is the treason of Sir Turquine, a knight so strong it seems no man can defeat him. He has imprisoned threescore and four of my bravest knights in his castle."

"I ride tomorrow to challenge him and free his captives," vowed Lancelot. "What is the second task?"

"Two giants hold the town of Whitmere in thrall," said Arthur.

"I will rout them both!" the knight boasted.

At dawn the Knight of the Lake rode
until he came to Sir Turquine's castle. From
the branches of a great oak dangled the shields
of Arthur's imprisoned knights. A brass basin
also hung from a branch. When Lancelot beat upon it
with his spear-end, Sir Turquine galloped forth.

"Who are you to beat so brazenly?" he demanded.

"I am the Knight of the Lake. I serve King Arthur."

"Then I will add your shield to yon tree," sneered Turquine.

Readying their lances, they spurred their horses as fast as
they could go. Each one's spear struck the other's shield with such
force that both men tumbled to the ground. Staggering to their
feet, they flung themselves at each other, raining fearsome blows
until both were equally battered and bruised.

At last Sir Turquine began to tire. Then Lancelot dealt him a
stunning blow. Sir Turquine sank to his knees and threw aside his
sword and shield. He said, "Fair knight, I see that you are the
greatest knight in all the world. For, until I met you, *I* was called
the mightiest."

When the Knight of the Lake freed Turquine's prisoners, they
begged him to return to Camelot with them. But he said,
"I have another service to perform for our king."

Lancelot rode for three days to the town of Whitmere. There he met a giant as tall as three men, who guarded the causeway that ran across a marsh to the town gates. The monster shook a club studded with iron spikes. "You shall not pass," he snarled.

"In the name of King Arthur, I order you to stand aside," said the Knight of the Lake, drawing his sword. "Or prepare to fight."

"I'll smash you, you boastful worm!" bellowed the giant, swinging his club so that it whistled past Lancelot's helmet. Wheeling his horse, the knight charged. One blow of his sword sheared the club in two. A second blow cut the giant's legs out from under him, and the creature fell into the marsh and sank beneath the mud.

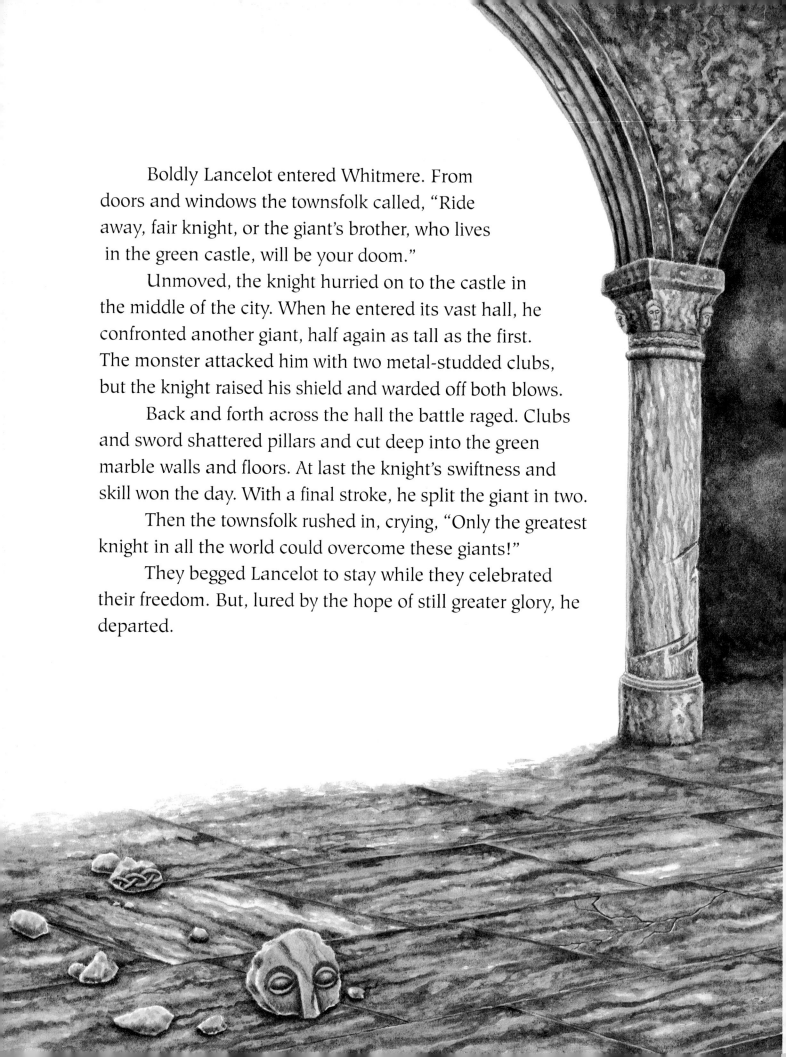

Boldly Lancelot entered Whitmere. From doors and windows the townsfolk called, "Ride away, fair knight, or the giant's brother, who lives in the green castle, will be your doom."

Unmoved, the knight hurried on to the castle in the middle of the city. When he entered its vast hall, he confronted another giant, half again as tall as the first. The monster attacked him with two metal-studded clubs, but the knight raised his shield and warded off both blows.

Back and forth across the hall the battle raged. Clubs and sword shattered pillars and cut deep into the green marble walls and floors. At last the knight's swiftness and skill won the day. With a final stroke, he split the giant in two.

Then the townsfolk rushed in, crying, "Only the greatest knight in all the world could overcome these giants!"

They begged Lancelot to stay while they celebrated their freedom. But, lured by the hope of still greater glory, he departed.

As Lancelot rode through a strange forest, he met a young woman on the path. She cried out, "Sir knight, I pray you to help my brother, who was wounded in the service of King Arthur. He lies on his deathbed, in our castle yonder. A wise woman told me that a bit of cloth from the altar of the Chapel Perilous will heal him. But the place is so dangerous, only the greatest knight in the world can bring back the cloth."

"Who are you?" asked the knight. "Who is your brother?"

"My name is Isabeau," the woman replied. "My brother is Sir Melyot."

"I know him," said the Knight of the Lake coldly. Melyot had accused him of being arrogant and lacking a knightly heart.

Isabeau's tearful eyes touched Lancelot and reminded him of Niniane's tears at their parting. But he pushed aside these tender thoughts. "I will go," he said, "to prove that I am rightly called the greatest knight in the world."

Lancelot reached the Chapel Perilous at sunset. All was silent. But when he pushed open the church doors, he saw thirty knights in black armor, each taller than a mortal man. With swords drawn, they glared and gnashed their teeth at him.

Beyond them, by the high altar, was a woman dressed in black; her face was hidden by dark veils. "Go, Knight of the Lake, or you will surely die," she warned.

Suddenly the black guards fell upon the knight with blows that jarred his bones and rattled his teeth; but his sword slid through them as harmlessly as though he fought empty air.

He battled bravely on until, exhausted by his struggle, he retreated to the churchyard. The veiled woman called after him, "There can be no victory for you here: only heartbreak and despair."

"My heart is diamond-hard," said the knight. "My spirit will not break."

Time after time he charged forward, only to be beaten back by the black soldiers. Their flesh was like mist, but they battered him with more than mortal power.

Tasting failure for the first time, Lancelot sat upon the chapel steps. He wept because he had failed to prove himself the greatest knight of all. But then a change came over him. He thought how selfish it was to weep for lost glory when lovely Isabeau must lose the brother she cherished. And Sir Melyot, who had served Arthur honorably, must lose his life. It no longer mattered that Melyot had called Lancelot arrogant and cold, for now he felt the truth of those words.

Lastly he thought of Niniane, whose kindness and love he had repaid with anger and harshness. "I wish that I could lay this victory at her feet to win her forgiveness," he said.

For the sake of these others and their sorrows, the knight wearily took up his sword and shield and reentered the Chapel Perilous.

Again the black company fell upon him. But to his amazement, their blows were now as harmless as puffs of air. Each thrust of his sword caused an enemy to melt away like mist in the morning sun.

Finally only the knight and the veiled woman remained. "You have passed the test," she said. Then she laughed sweetly.

"Why do you mock me?" he demanded.

"I laugh with joy," she said, "to see that you have found your second heart. You have become a knight who is both brave and generous, who will serve the mightiest king or the weakest of the weak. You can rightly be called the greatest knight of all."

With these words, she drew aside her veil. Then the astonished knight beheld Niniane, the Lady of the Lake.

"Were the black guardians a false danger?" he asked.

"No," the enchantress replied, "but they are a threat only to unworthy knights. And the danger to good Sir Melyot is also real. We must take a piece of the altar cloth to cure him."

So Lancelot took his sword and cut off a piece of the white linen. Then, both seated upon his charger, they returned to the castle where anxious Isabeau tended her brother.

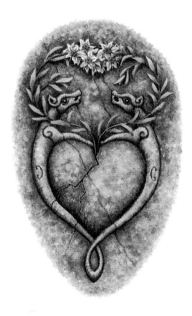

When the cloth was laid upon his breast, Melyot was healed. The four rode to Camelot, where Niniane addressed King Arthur, Queen Guinevere, and all the company of the Round Table. "I present to you the son of King Ban and Queen Helen of Benwick, who was my charge," she told them. "His name is Lancelot."

"Henceforward you will be known as Sir Lancelot of the Lake," said Arthur.

His name restored, Lancelot became the greatest champion of the Round Table—a knight fearless and tender, true to the two hearts that beat as one in his chest.

AUTHOR'S NOTE

While I have compressed and edited events, this story follows in outline and incident traditional accounts of Lancelot's early days. Among numerous volumes consulted, the most helpful include *Lancelot of the Lake*, translated by Corin Corley, based on the Old French *Lancelot do Lac* (Oxford, England: Oxford University Press, 1989); *The Legends of King Arthur and His Knights*, compiled and arranged by Sir James Knowles (London and New York: Frederick Warne and Co., 1862); *The Story of the Champions of the Round Table*, written and illustrated by Howard Pyle (New York: Charles Scribner's Sons, 1905; reissued, New York: Dover Publications, 1968); *King Arthur and His Knights of the Round Table*, Roger Lancelyn Green (London: Puffin Books/The Penguin Group, 1953); and *Stories of King Arthur*, retold by Blanche Winder (New York: Airmont Publishing Company, 1968).

A Doubleday Book for Young Readers

Published by Delacorte Press
Bantam Doubleday Dell Publishing Group, Inc.
1540 Broadway, New York, New York 10036

Doubleday and the portrayal of an anchor with a dolphin are trademarks of Bantam Doubleday Dell Publishing Group, Inc.

The text of this book is set in 14-point Hiroshige.
Book design by Kimberly M. Adlerman

Library of Congress Cataloging-in-Publication Data

San Souci, Robert D.
  Young Lancelot / by Robert D. San Souci ; illustrated by Jamichael Henterly
    p. cm.
  Includes bibliographical references (p. 11).
  Summary: Presents the life of Lancelot, relating how he became the greatest knight of the Round Table.
  ISBN 0–385–32171–6 (alk. paper)
  1. Lancelot (Legendary character)—Legends. [1. Lancelot (Legendary character)—Legends. 2. Knights and knighthood—Folklore. 3. Folklore—England.] I. Henterly, Jamichael, ill. II. Title.
PZ8. 1.S227Y1 1996
398.2′0942′02—dc20   95–21361
                                              CIP
                                              AC

Manufactured in the United States of America
November 1996
10 9 8 7 6 5 4 3 2 1